For the birds

—Bette and Michi

 Published in the United States by Random House Children's Books, a division of Penguin Random House LLC, New York.
Random House and the colophon are registered trademarks of Penguin Random House LLC.
Visit us on the Web! rhcbooks.com
Educators and librarians, for a variety of teaching tools, visit us at RHTeachersLibrarians.com
Library of Congress Cataloging-in-Publication Data is available upon request.
ISBN 978-0-593-17676-4 (trade) — ISBN 978-0-593-17677-1 (lib. bdg.) — ISBN 978-0-593-17678-8 (ebook)
The text is set in 16-point P22 Platten Neu Pro. Book design by Nicole de las Heras
MANUFACTURED IN ITALY 10 9 8 7 6 5 4 3 2 1 First Edition
Random House Children's Books supports the First Amendment and celebrates the right to read.

The Tale of the Mandarin Duck

A Modern Fable

story by
Bette Midler

photographs and afterword by
Michiko Kakutani

with illustrations by Joana Avillez

Random House New York

This is a story
of rare birds—
both feathered
and human.

Once upon a time, not very long ago, there was a great city, built on an island, that was famous for its people.

There were many kinds of people living there: artists and writers; salespeople and stockbrokers; people who worked with their hands; butchers, bakers, and perfume makers; people who drove cabs, trucks, and trains; people who fixed streets and cleaned streets.

So many different kinds of people doing so many different things!

But no matter what they did, these people were world famous for their liveliness.

They talked to each other everywhere: in elevators, on subways, in restaurants.

They would gather in little groups on street corners and tell each other jokes, or discuss the daily news of their city and laugh uproariously.

They yelled, sang, and generally had a good time.

They looked each other in the eye, and pretty much liked what they saw.

Information

A new bird came to town.

No one had ever seen a bird like this. Many birds are very beautiful, but this bird was extraordinary! He was a Mandarin Duck. When bird lovers heard he was in the pond, they ran to see him.

Word spread about the duck, and soon people began flocking to look at him. Wouldn't you?

It was the most exciting thing to happen to the city in a long time.

How did this duck get there?

Where did he come from?

Who was this duck?

The crowds were immense.

Everyone had their phones up, taking pictures of the Mandarin Duck.

Then she put her phone away and just watched the Mandarin Duck be what he was: something so rare that he had to be seen with your own two eyes, and remembered with your heart.

So the grown-ups put their phones down, too . . . and just watched.

They watched long and hard. What an effect this bird had on people! They just LOVED him.

Soon after that, the people put their phones away.

Their old habits returned.

They talked, they laughed, and sometimes they even sang.

They looked each other in the eye and pretty much liked what they saw.

And all

because of

the Mandarin Duck.

Then one day . . .

. . . the Mandarin Duck flew away.

Everyone missed him, but he had worked his magic. He had reminded the people in the city—the artists and writers, the butchers, bakers, and perfume makers, and everyone else—to look at the world with their own two eyes. And if they did, they would see that all around them are rare and beautiful birds, with and without feathers.

WHY A DUCK?

by Michiko Kakutani

He arrived in the city with the autumn leaves, just as the trees in Central Park were turning red and gold.

It was the fall of 2018, and New York City quickly fell in love with the Mandarin Duck—this mysterious, rainbow-colored bird, who looked like a visitor from another planet.

Who was this duck? And where had he come from?

Some fans thought he was a former pet. Others thought he was a fugitive from a local zoo or an upstate farm. One little boy wondered what sort of batteries he ran on, lithium or solar-powered? "He's so beautiful," one woman said, "it's hard to believe he's real."

Pictures of the duck soon went viral on Twitter and Instagram. *New York* magazine dubbed him the "Hot Duck" and the city's "most eligible bachelor." The *New York Times* compared him to a punk rocker, while the *Los Angeles Times* likened him to a cubist painting.

Twitter's Manhattan Bird Alert and the news site Gothamist tracked the duck's whereabouts, as both tourists and New Yorkers flocked to his favorite haunts. It wasn't long before China's largest newspaper, the *People's Daily,* tweeted a photo of him, CNN sent TV cameras to film him, and the *Guardian* reported that "Mandarin mania" had taken over New York City.

Although the duck took some trips to other parts of Manhattan—and was even sighted across the river in New Jersey—he always returned to the pond in Central Park. That is, until one day in March, when he disappeared as suddenly as he'd arrived.

Those of us who loved visiting him in the park felt a sense of abandonment. We felt like Tony Soprano did when the duck family left his backyard swimming pool and flew away. We worried about the duck. We wondered whether he'd gone north for the summer, or found a mate and moved to the suburbs.

Mandarin Ducks are native to East Asia, and for centuries they have been depicted in folktales and poems in Japan and China as symbols of love, devotion, and grace. Veteran birdwatcher David Barrett, who runs the Manhattan Bird Alert on Twitter, doesn't know what happened to our duck, but reminds us that the bird's visit made "thousands of people happy in dark times."

That's something to be grateful for, even as many of us hope that the duck might make a return visit next fall—or maybe the fall after that.